Disney

Beauty and the Beast

Ladybird

A handsome young prince once lived in a magnificent castle. Although he had everything he could wish for, he was selfish, spoilt and unkind.

One cold winter's night an old beggar woman came to the castle seeking shelter. But the Prince refused to help her. He said she was ugly and sent her away.

"Do not be deceived by appearances," warned the old woman. "True beauty is found within!" And she turned at once into a beautiful enchantress. To punish the Prince for his cruelty, she changed him into a hideous beast and cast a spell on the castle and everyone in it.

Then she gave the Prince two gifts: a magic mirror, which would show him anything he asked, and an enchanted rose, which would bloom until his twenty-first birthday. If by then he could learn to love, and earn a girl's love in return, the spell would be broken. If not, he would remain a Beast *for ever*.

In a village near the castle a beautiful young girl named Belle lived with her father, an eccentric inventor named Maurice. Belle was kind and gentle, and she loved to read. Her favourite books were romantic stories about kings and queens, princes and princesses.

The handsomest man in the village was named Gaston. He was also the most conceited man, because all the girls adored him – and he knew it!

As soon as he saw Belle, he decided he would marry *her*, and no one else. "She's the best-looking girl in town," Gaston told his friend Lefou. "And only the best is good enough for me!"

One morning Gaston, closely followed by Lefou, came up to Belle as she left the village bookshop. "Hello, Belle," he said.

"Oh, hello, Gaston," she replied, turning back to her book.

Gaston snatched the book from her hand. "Girls shouldn't read," he told her. "You should pay attention to more important things – like *me*! Come with me to the tavern, and I'll show you my hunting trophies!"

But Belle wasn't interested. "I have to get home to help my father," she said.

At that moment – BOOOM! – a huge explosion shook the ground, and a plume of smoke rose in the air. It was coming from Belle's cottage!

"Papa!" cried Belle, running home as fast as she could.

Luckily, Maurice was all right. But his newest invention wasn't.

"I'll never get this contraption to work!" he said, giving the machine a kick.

"Oh, yes, you will," said Belle soothingly. "And you'll win first prize at the fair tomorrow!"

"Do you think so?" asked Maurice uncertainly. Then cheered by Belle's encouragement, he picked up his tools and went back to work. He soon had his invention mended and running perfectly.

Next morning Belle helped Maurice to load his new machine and hitch the wagon to their family horse, Philippe. Maurice pulled his cloak around him, climbed onto Philippe's back and set off.

"Goodbye, Papa!" Belle called. "Good luck at the fair!"

Maurice had a long way to travel, and the route was unfamiliar to him. By nightfall he was lost in the forest. Suddenly a pack of hungry wolves appeared.

Philippe reared up frightened, overturning the wagon, and the old man was thrown to the ground. As his horse galloped away in terror, Maurice desperately tried to save himself from the wolves.

Seeing a light ahead of him, Maurice ran towards it with all his might. Just when he thought he could go no further, he found himself within the gates of a huge, gloomy castle. Sighing with relief, he realised he was safe – for now.

Inside the castle Maurice was astonished to discover that he was surrounded by enchanted objects. There was an officious clock called Cogsworth and an elegant candelabra called Lumiere.

Cogsworth was uncertain about letting Maurice stay. "The Master will be furious," he said.

"The Master doesn't need to know," Lumiere replied.

Suddenly the door flew open. Maurice gasped in terror as a huge, monstrous beast strode into the room and towered over him.

"Strangers are not welcome here!" roared the Beast.

"He was lost in the woods," Lumiere explained. "He was cold and wet, so…"

"RRRRRAAAAGGGGGHHH!" The force of the Beast's roar blew out every one of Lumiere's candles.

Cogsworth peeped out from under the carpet. "Master, I was against it from the start," he said. "But he needed a place to stay."

"I'll give him a place to stay!" shouted the Beast. "Lock him in the tower!"

Next morning Gaston went to see Belle. He was determined to get her to marry him. He had even brought a priest – and half the village had come to watch!

But Belle refused Gaston's proposal and sent him away.

As Belle shut the door, Gaston stumbled over the doorstep and ended up in a puddle. His eyes blazed with rage and humiliation, and the crowd fell silent.

"She turned you down, huh?" said Lefou.

Gaston stood up. "Of course not," he said. "She's just playing hard to get!" But under his breath, he muttered, "Nobody turns me down. One way or another, I'm going to have Belle for my wife!"

A short time later Belle was surprised to see Philippe returning home alone.

"Where's Papa?" she cried. "What's happened?" The horse just whinnied anxiously.

"Take me to him, Philippe!" said Belle, jumping onto his back. The faithful horse galloped down the road and into the forest, to the place where he had left Maurice. In the distance Belle could see the castle. She ran towards it.

Belle was terrified. She had never seen such a horrible place, even in her worst nightmares.

The castle seemed empty, but once inside Belle could see the flickering light of a candelabra. She followed it through the murky corridors and up to the tower, calling, "Papa, where are you?" At last she found her father in a cold, dark cell. "Oh, Papa!" she cried. "We must get you out of here!"

Suddenly she felt darkness settling over her. Belle turned in terror to find it was the Beast. "Who are you?" she asked.

"The Master of this castle," replied the Beast softly.

"Your father was trespassing," he continued. "He is my prisoner now."

"Please let him go," begged Belle. "Take me instead!"

The Beast stared at Belle. He had never met anyone so beautiful and unselfish. "Very well," he said, "but you must promise to stay here for ever."

"Belle, no!" cried Maurice. "I won't let you do it!"

Belle bravely turned to the Beast. "You have my word," she said.

The Beast dragged Maurice from his cell and sent him back to the village.

Later that night a wet, weary and wild-eyed Maurice burst into the tavern where Gaston and his friends were drinking.

"Help!" he cried. "A huge, monstrous beast has Belle locked up in his castle! You must help me to rescue her!"

Everyone burst out laughing. They knew Maurice was strange, but now he seemed positively insane! Amidst hoots and jeers, two men threw the old man out into the street.

Gaston, who had been laughing with the others, suddenly grew quiet. "You know," he whispered to Lefou, "that crazy old man has given me an idea. I think I know how to make Belle my bride! Listen to my plan…"

Back at the castle, the Beast had shown Belle to her room. She had followed him down the stairs and through a maze of corridors until they arrived at a luxurious bedroom, where the Beast left her alone.

But Belle didn't notice the splendour around her. She threw herself down on the bed and sobbed, thinking she would never see her father or her home again.

Suddenly someone spoke! Belle looked up in surprise to find Mrs Potts, an enchanted teapot, and her son Chip, a teacup. Together with a friendly wardrobe, they did everything they could to cheer her up. And soon Belle began to feel better.

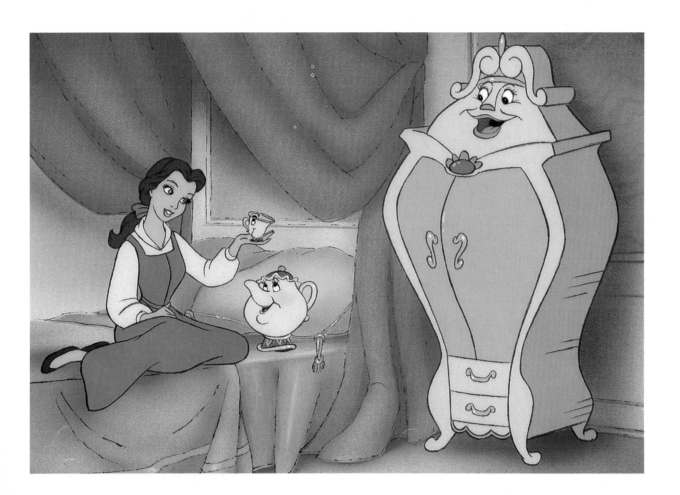

That evening the Beast invited Belle to dinner. But when Cogsworth announced that dinner was served, Belle refused to go downstairs.

Outside the dining room window, snow was falling. In the room, a fire glowed warmly and the table was set with the finest china. Mrs Potts stood beside Lumiere, watching the Beast pace up and down. "What's taking her so long?" he growled.

"Do try to be patient, Sir," said Mrs Potts.

"Master," said Lumiere, "have you thought that perhaps this girl could be the one to break the spell?"

"Of course I have!" the Beast roared. "I'm not a fool! But it's no use. She's so beautiful and I… well, she won't even look at me! I don't know what to do."

"You could start by making yourself more presentable," said Mrs Potts. "Try to act like a gentleman. Be kind and sincere."

"Shower her with compliments," suggested Lumiere. "Give her a smile or two."

Then they both spoke at the same time. "Above all, you must control your temper!"

KNOCK! KNOCK! KNOCK! Thinking it was Belle, the Beast looked up and tried hard to smile as the door opened. But it was only Cogsworth.

"Well, where is she?" demanded the Beast.

"Er… who?" said Cogsworth, trying not to appear nervous. "Oh yes, you mean the girl. Well…"

The Beast glared at him impatiently. Cogsworth knew he had to tell the truth. "She's not coming. She says she isn't hungry."

The Beast turned in fury and thundered out of the room. "Fine!" he yelled. "Then she can go ahead and starve. If she won't eat with me, then she won't eat at all."

And as he spoke a petal fell from the wilting rose on his table and fluttered slowly to the bottom of the jar. The pile of shrivelled petals was growing bigger every day.

A few hours later Belle timidly crept out of her room and found her way to the kitchen. Mrs Potts and Chip were there, and so were Cogsworth and Lumiere. They had been talking about Belle, wondering what they could do to help her like the Beast.

"Mademoiselle," said Lumiere, "is there anything we can do to make your stay more comfortable?"

"Well…" confessed Belle, "I am a little hungry."

That was all they needed to hear. The stove began to cook. Mrs Potts woke the crockery and cutlery, and Lumiere directed the meal as if it were a wonderful show. Even Cogsworth, who was nervous at first about disobeying their master's orders, joined in the fun.

When it was all over, Belle cheered with delight. "That was magnificent! And it was delicious! Thank you!" Then she added, "Do you think I could have a look round the castle?"

Cogsworth and Lumiere took Belle on a tour, showing her each room in detail. But when they came to a wide staircase, they stopped.

"What's up there?" asked Belle.

"That is the West Wing," Cogsworth explained, "and it is forbidden."

Belle was curious about the West Wing, and when Cogsworth and Lumiere weren't looking, she raced up the stairs on her own.

At the end of a long, gloomy corridor, she found a dark, disorderly room filled with broken furniture, cracked mirrors and torn paintings. Dirty clothes were strewn everywhere, and chewed-up bones were heaped in a corner. It was the Beast's lair.

On a table near the window, Belle spotted the magic rose. Its petals were beginning to droop, but it still sparkled. She was just reaching out to touch it when the Beast leapt in through a broken window.

"RAARRGGH!" he roared furiously. "What are you doing here? Get out! GET OUT!"

Belle fled in terror.

She found Philippe and galloped off into the woods. But they hadn't travelled far before they were attacked by hungry wolves.

Just as the wolves closed in for the kill, the Beast appeared. Fighting savagely, he beat off the wolves and they limped away. The Beast then collapsed, wounded.

Belle knew that this was her chance to escape. But she chose instead to help the Beast back to the castle and tend his wounds. "Thank you for saving my life," she said quietly.

From then on, everything started to change between Belle and the Beast.

The Beast lost some of his gruffness, and Belle began to see a sweet, soft side to his nature. Soon she was no longer afraid of him. To the delight of everyone in the household, they were becoming friends.

Belle also became his teacher. He didn't know how to eat with a knife and fork, so she taught him. He didn't know how to read, so she read to him. She showed him how to feed birds, and how to play in the snow.

One evening the Beast asked Belle if she was happy. "Yes," she said, "but I miss my father. I wish there were some way I could see him again."

"There is," said the Beast, showing her the magic mirror.

What Belle saw in the mirror chilled her heart. Her father was wandering alone in the forest looking for her! "I must go and help him," she cried.

The Beast agreed, though it broke his heart to do so, for he was in love with Belle. "Take the mirror," he told her, "so you can look back and remember me."

"Oh, thank you!" said Belle, then she rushed out to saddle Philippe.

Belle found her father, soaked and feverish, lying in the snow. She quickly took him home to their cottage, where she nursed him back to health.

Soon after Maurice had recovered, Gaston, Lefou and a crowd of the villagers gathered outside the cottage. The director of the local asylum knocked at the door. "Your father is insane," he told Belle. "He was raving about some beast. For your own safety, I have come to take your father away, unless you agree to marry Gaston."

"Never! My father's not insane!" cried Belle. "The Beast is real! I can prove it!" She held the magic mirror before the crowd. "Show me the Beast!" she commanded.

When the people saw the Beast, they began to scream in terror. But, angry that his plan had failed, Gaston grabbed the mirror. "This Beast is a danger to us all!" he shouted. "Who'll come with me to kill him?"

The frenzied crowd followed Gaston into the forest. Guided by the mirror, they soon reached the Beast's castle. Cogsworth, Lumiere and the others bravely tried to fight them off, but Gaston pushed past them. He made his way up to the Beast's lair and forced him out onto a high balcony. The Beast, miserable without Belle, hardly fought back. As they struggled, the Beast suddenly heard Belle's voice.

"You came back!" he cried, turning to face her. At that moment, Gaston plunged a large dagger into the Beast's back.

Howling with pain, the Beast furiously grasped his attacker's arm. Gaston dropped his weapon and the Beast let go. Gaston stepped back, slipped – and tumbled down to his death.

As the Beast collapsed in agony, Belle rushed to his side. "No! You can't die," she sobbed. "I love you!"

All at once a magical glow filled the air. Belle watched in wonder as the Beast was transformed into a strong, handsome young prince.

"Belle," the Prince said softly, "it's me!"

Belle looked into the Prince's eyes, and saw the warm, gentle eyes of the Beast she loved. She smiled radiantly at the Prince as he took her in his arms.

The enchantress's spell had been broken at last! The gloomy castle was turned back into a beautiful, shining palace with lush green meadows and a moat of deep blue water. Everywhere was filled with laughter and singing, as the sun shone brightly.

Cogsworth, Lumiere and Mrs Potts changed back into the humans they had once been, and Belle's father returned to the castle as if by magic. They watched with joy as Belle and the Prince shared a tender kiss.

For Belle and the Prince, a new life of love and happiness was just beginning.